YALEY

by

L. Vincent

First edition published March 2021

All production design are trademarks
For information regarding bulk purchases of this book, digital purchase and special discounts, please contact the author

ISBN 978-1-6780-5441-0

On the first morning of autumn, Yaley wandered away from her village to dance under the stars like she had done many nights since her parents passed away. They had told her stories about elephants, and most nights Yaley imagined the elephants were watching her dance. One night she even thought she spotted one creeping in the bushes.

"Yaley, get back here now!" her brother Dev called.

1

"Your sneaking away to that clearing by yourself is dangerous," Yaley's grandmother scolded as she caught Yaley walking through the door. "Do you know what kind of beasts could attack you out there? You've seen the elephants surrounding these parts."

"They won't hurt me," Yaley said with certainty.

"Do they know that?" Dev questioned. "And even if they don't, King Norman's men probably will. We heard more news this morning of them demanding payments from a village nearby. They are getting closer to Candor."

"You don't think they'll actually come here, do you? We don't have much to offer them," Yaley's little sister Ari quivered.

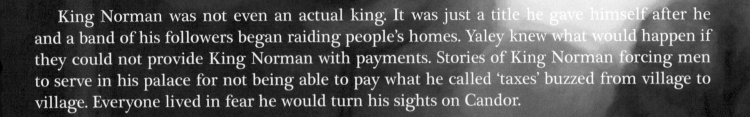

King Norman was not even an actual king. It was just a title he gave himself after he and a band of his followers began raiding people's homes. Yaley knew what would happen if they could not provide King Norman with payments. Stories of King Norman forcing men to serve in his palace for not being able to pay what he called 'taxes' buzzed from village to village. Everyone lived in fear he would turn his sights on Candor.

The next morning before dawn, Yaley snuck away once again to dance with the crisp fall air and fading moonlight. It was then she finally caught him in her gaze.

He was more beautiful than all of the sunsets in Candor. Despite all her senses telling her not to, Yaley could not resist reaching out to touch him. "Have you been watching me, sweet boy?"

He was smaller than any of the elephants she had ever seen wandering around her village.

"Do you feel that too?" His trunk met her displays of affection. "You know you make me nervous when you watch me dance, but you also make me calm. Calm like when my parents use to watch me dance. Calm from loving so much."

"May I call you Love?" Yaley asked. He let out a booming trumpet, making her giggle. She took his response as a yes.
Then Yaley heard screaming in the distance.
"I have to go, but I'll be back soon, Love." He released her.

By the time she reached the village, she could see a raid taking place. King Norman's soldiers had finally come for Candor.

"I'm sorry, but it's all we have," cried Yaley's grandmother. "You can't take him! There must be something else we can offer you."

King Norman was nowhere to be seen, but his men had Dev in their grip.

Sorrow swept through the village. King Norman's soldiers had taken most of the food in Candor, but Yaley only felt despair over what could not be replaced. Silent tears fell from her grandmother's face and no amount of coddling could stop her sister's sobbing.

Yaley soon found herself in the same place she had gone to the morning after her parents died. The clearing provided no music to dance to except the wind and silent presence of her ancestors. It was all she ever needed.

Love must have sensed Yaley's mounting frustration and he suddenly appeared to her. The comfort of his presence felt like home.

"Love, what am I to do?" Tears had finally escaped Yaley's eyes.

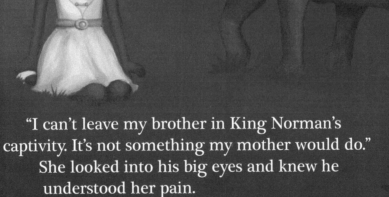

"I can't leave my brother in King Norman's captivity. It's not something my mother would do." She looked into his big eyes and knew he understood her pain.

The plan Yaley devised that night would take some convincing in her village, especially with her grandmother.

"Are you mad, girl? King Norman has dozens of men protecting him and that ugly palace. How can we possibly get your brother back?" Grandmother's voice rose.

"I am mad. His men took my brother and I won't spend my days crying over it," Yaley retorted. "I will get him back for us. Our ancestors would never have settled for this injustice and neither should we."

Grandmother released the first boisterous laugh Yaley had heard in years. "Well, child, if you are that certain, I will help you convince the women of Candor. I only fear for your safety if it doesn't work."

The next evening, Grandmother had gathered all of the women in Candor to hear
Yaley's plan. They were in no mood to listen to a young girl's reckless ideas, but they knew
to respect Grandmother's request.

"Norman is not our king. We owe him nothing. He's just a thief. We may not be able to
get our food back, but will we let him keep the men of Candor as prisoners?" Yaley asked
them.

The women's heads fell. "I am leaving for Baleful at dawn to plea with him. I ask you all
to come with me. If you choose not to, I will understand."

Yaley felt the next part of her
plan would be easier to
enact. Love stood in
waiting outside the
village as though
he sensed her request
coming.
"I need your help, Love," Yaley
said, without even realizing she already had it.

The villagers gaped in awe at Yaley and the dozens of elephants she returned with as daylight broke.

"This is your plan? To have us torn apart by these deadly brutes?" a woman cried.

"These gentle beasts won't harm you. Can you say the same for Norman and his men?" Yaley reached out to embrace Love. Without hesitation he knelt to hoist her onto his back with his trunk.

Everyone looked on astonished. Elephants in Candor were rumored to be more deadly than puff adders and hippopotamuses, and yet this young girl had tamed one.

"They will follow you," Grandmother announced and while the women remained silent, Yaley knew they had agreed.

Yaley led every able-bodied young woman down the winding path to Baleful. It would be days before they would ever reach it and she had no idea what she would do once they finally did. Yaley thought Norman would have even less interest in listening to her than the people of Candor originally did, but she knew she would not meet his violence with violence if their encounter demanded it.

The women had left Candor with little food and grew weary with each passing day.
Yaley feared they would not make it but could see them growing strong in other ways.
Each woman was determined only to return to Candor once the men were free.

The sun began to fall when they came across a burning village with women sitting atop a hill.

"We have to ride on. The fire could spook the elephants." They exchanged concerned looks.

"We can't leave them to suffer. Let the elephants rest here while I speak with them," Yaley said.

The women of the village regarded her with caution. "Are you a servant of Norman?"

"No, I travelled from Candor after he pillaged my home and took my brother," Yaley explained. "The other women from my village ride with me to Baleful to rescue all of the men taken from our homes."

"King Norman took my brother and my father," a small child said through tears.

An elderly woman emerged from the smoke, covered in burns. "We refused to give him our food, so he set fire to our homes and took our men in the night."

"What is this village called?" asked Yaley.

"Mount Volition. Where are these women you say you came here with?"

Yaley pointed to the bottom of the hill. The
women looked in shock at how
naturally they sat among such
menacing animals. Yaley had not
noticed Love trailed behind her
up to Mount Volition.
    The villagers gathered into a huddle and
spoke in a hushed whisper before turning back
to Yaley.
    "We did not allow Norman to have our summer rations
that were hidden, so we will share them with you and your
people if you allow us to travel under your protection to free
our men as well. It's clearly been some time since you all have
eaten well," the elderly woman observed.
    "We will accept your assistance, but you must understand no one of Mount
Volition or Candor is allowed to do any physical harm to Norman, nor the men
in his service."
    The women returned skeptical glances but nodded in acceptance.

The villagers of Mount Volition showed them
to a nearby watering hole where they watered the
elephants and regained their strength. Yaley was grateful. The food they supplied
would be enough to get them through their journey.

The women were less than two miles away from Baleful when they saw Norman's monstrous palace. It sat there surrounded by battered and bruised men adding more to its large structure. Yaley searched for Dev in the sea of faces working away at another man's dream but didn't see him.

They had decided to stop there and try to meet with Norman in the morning. The sun had barely risen the next day when ten gaunt, young men rode up to them on horses.

"King Norman wants to know what business you have here?" one of the men inquired.

"He has my brother. I want to negotiate a trade," Yaley stepped forward.

Later, Norman met them along the perimeter of Baleful. He was a slender man in ornate clothing, and hundreds of men stood at his back in fear. Yaley still could not find her brother's face.

"Who wishes to trade with me?" Norman hissed.

Yaley climbed down from Love's back, whispering into his ear. Then she announced, "I am Yaley of Candor. I have come to negotiate my brother's freedom and the freedom of the other men being held here against their will."

"Why would I ever negotiate with a girl?" he smirked. "What could you possibly have to offer me?"

"The elephants," said Yaley. "They could better serve your palace and conquest than the men of Candor and Mount Volition. My companions and I have proven they can be controlled."

The temptation of her offer showed in his eyes. Nevertheless, he let out a resounding "No."

"Then I'll fight you." She stood her ground. "I'll fight you for their freedom. Just me and you."

Norman belted out the loudest laugh Yaley had ever heard.

"You send other men to do your fighting," she locked eyes with him, "so why not fight on your own for once? And if you do win, you can have the elephants and we will return back to what's left of our homes without our families."

"What's to stop me from taking the elephants and your companions for my service now?" his voice was filled with fury at her challenge.

Honkkkkk! Honkkk! Honkkkk!

The elephants reacted to his rage. Yaley grinned and caressed Love's trunk.

"They are loyal creatures. They will not submit easily. Only I can sway them."

His desire to not look weak in front of the men was clear. He turned to address the crowd. "I will accept the girl's challenge."

The duel would take place at dawn in Norman's newly built fighting pit.

"Why would you do that? You said no violence," the women asked when they returned to camp.

"It's the only type of negotiation he understands. I had to compromise," explained Yaley.

"Have you ever fought anyone before? Let alone a man?"

"No, but I have to at least try for Dev. I won't go back to Candor without him." Tears filled Yaley's eyes. The pain of the journey she endured since Norman's men invaded her village overcame her at once.

They all ate in silence before falling into a worried slumber. Love guarded Yaley's side the entire night and his presence gave her the reassurance she needed. She knew that after tomorrow, everything would be fine.

The fighting pit was large and imposing. Yaley had never seen this many people in one place, let alone there to see her. Norman came dressed in his best attire, completely adorned in gold and purple embroidered silks. He looked as though he was prepared for a performance instead of a fight.

Yaley scanned the audience around them hoping to catch sight of Love, despite knowing she would not. The parade of elephants were not permitted in the pit. The women of the pillaged villages sat in the front row. Yaley could feel the anticipation radiating off them. She gave up looking for her brother in the crowd. Her reason for being there was greater than her family.

Three valets walked into the middle arena carrying an assortment of weaponry.

"Each fighter may choose one."

Norman plucked out a shiny, gold-enameled, doubled-edged spear encrusted with purple gemstones that matched his silks. When the weapons were then offered to her, she nodded her head in refusal.

Two of the valets exited the arena. Norman cackled.

"The girl thinks she can beat me empty-handed! After this is over, I will find a way to reward her confidence," he yelled to the spectators.

They readied their positions, then the valet gestured to Yaley and Norman, signaling the start of the fight. Norman charged at Yaley immediately. He swung powerful blows but failed to hit her. Yaley moved swiftly, as though she were dancing, easily avoiding the swing of his spear.

She could see the frustration growing on his face. The crowd roared. She danced around him for minutes without ever touching him once. Norman began to lose his breath as they picked up the speed of him swinging and her dodging.

"You stupid girl. Stop playing and fight me!"

It seemed odd to Yaley how natural this interaction felt. She moved like she was by herself in the clearing just outside of Candor and not in a stadium with hundreds of eyes upon her. Riding bareback on Love for days had strengthened her body enough to go the distance in this battle against Norman.

It was in that moment of hope she finally spotted him. Yaley's eyes found Dev sitting in the stands.

As Yaley looked at Dev, she did not notice the rock lying behind her. She stepped back to avoid Norman's next blow and tripped, landing on her back.

Norman readied his spear to drive it through her and end their little dance. He thrusted it with great force and Yaley rolled out of the way to evade the lunge. The spear buried itself in the ground beside her just as Norman tripped over the same rock, impaling himself on the other end of his spear.

No one expected Yaley of Candor to emerge victorious from the fighting pit of Baleful, but the entire stadium stormed the arena and lifted her high in celebration. In all the chaos and joy, she heard Love's trumpeting in celebration just outside the gates.

29

CPSIA information can be obtained
at www.ICGtesting.com
Printed in the USA
BVHW061544061221
623343BV00004B/50

* 9 7 8 1 6 7 8 0 5 4 4 1 0 *